AMZAT AND HIS BROTHERS

A Richard Jackson Book

AMZAT and HIS BROTHERS

Three Italian Tales

Remembered by Floriano Vecchi

and Retold by

PAULA FOX

Illustrations by Emily Arnold McCully

ORCHARD BOOKS   New York

Orchard Books, 95 Madison Avenue, New York, NY 10016

Manufactured in the United States of America
Book design by Mina Greenstein

The text of this book is set in 14 point Cochin.
The illustrations are rendered in pen-and-ink.
1   3   5   7   9   10   8   6   4   2

Library of Congress Cataloging-in-Publication Data
Fox, Paula.
Amzat and his brothers : three Italian tales / remembered by Floriano Vecchi
and retold by Paula Fox ; illustrations by Emily Arnold McCully.
p.   cm.   Contents: Amzat and his brothers — Mezgalten —
Olimpia, Cucol, and the door.
ISBN 0-531-05462-4.   ISBN 0-531-08612-7 (lib. bdg.)
1. Tales — Italy.   [1. Folklore — Italy.]   I. Vecchi, Floriano.   II. McCully, Emily
Arnold, ill.   III. Title.   PZ8.1.F8184Am   1993
398.2′0945 — dc20   [E]   92-19494

For Jennifer Theresa Sigerson

Preface

Every community of people, whether it is a nation or a tribe, has a treasury of folktales. These tales are a kind of unwritten library that is passed from generation to generation.

If you read folktales, you will notice that there is one theme common to all of them. It is the way human beings — sometimes disguised as animals — using their cleverness and courage and imagination, outwit their foes and turn misfortune into fortune.

The three stories in this book were told to me by Floriano Vecchi, who was born in Italy in a small village called Pianoro Vecchio in the Apennine Mountains not far from the city of Bologna.

When Floriano was a little boy, he spent a good deal of time with his grandfather, who had a farm in Pianoro

Vecchio. His grandfather was an herbalist as well as a farmer, and he was often away for days at a time, searching for medicinal herbs, which grew on the higher slopes of the mountains.

The herbs were very valuable: they had healing properties, and pharmacies in Bologna were eager to buy them.

When his grandfather returned from his quest for herbs, he would gather Floriano and his cousins to the barn. There, in the warm and comforting presence of the farm animals, in the light of a candle or two, the children would listen to the old man tell the old stories.

Floriano's grandfather was born in the middle of the last century, around 1850. That was before Italy became a unified country. The grandfather had heard the stories from his own grandfather. You can see how far back in time the stories stretch. They are like a great rope that ties the generations together.

The stories change a little with each teller. Details are added; even new characters may appear. Floriano's great-great-grandfather told them one way, his grandfather another, and as Floriano told them to me in New York City, so far from Pianoro Vecchio, he probably added a few things and changed others.

I, in my turn, have done the same.

Floriano still remembers the chestnuts and hazelnuts his grandfather sometimes brought to him when he returned to his farm. Floriano had to work hard to open the nuts with his small hands to get at the delicious smoky kernels. In the same way, we must work at memory to find the stories that have comforted, startled, made merry, and perhaps taught some human wisdom to the countless generations of people who have told and heard them.

When Floriano returned to his village in 1946, after the end of World War II, there was nothing left of Pianoro Vecchio. It had been bombed into rubble and dust. A new village was being built of steel and cement. It was not like the old stone village.

Cities and villages can be destroyed by wars as well as by catastrophes of nature like earthquakes and floods. But it seems that stories do not disappear. They last longer than anything else.

To be human is to be in a story.

Contents

AMZAT AND HIS BROTHERS

1

MEZGALTEN

27

OLIMPIA, CUCOL,
AND THE DOOR

45

Amzat and His Brothers

ALONG, LONG TIME AGO, two angry brothers named Ingrato and Bramoso lived with their angry wives, Tètra and Furiosa, in an old, cold, stone farmhouse in a dark, deep valley.

The brothers were angry because their donkey brayed in the middle of the night and woke them up, because their flock of geese honked all day long and gave them no peace, because their chickens ate huge quantities of corn but rarely laid an egg, and because their suppers were nearly always cold since the wood they used in their stove was too damp to catch fire.

But mostly they were angry because a very steep hill cast its long black shadow over their land the livelong day. As everyone knows, nothing much can grow in the earth without sun to warm the seeds.

So the two angry brothers and their two angry wives were forced to earn their daily bread by raising knobby, angry little sheep.

The sheep were angry because they were always chilly. No sooner did their fleece become thick than the brothers sheared them and took the wool to a village miles away to sell it.

On the very top of the steep hill that hid the sun and kept its rays from shining on the valley lived the third and youngest brother. His name was Amzat, and his wife was called Allegra, and they were cheerful from morning to dusk.

They had a fig tree, five olive trees, and a peach tree among whose branches a nightingale sometimes came to sing in the early spring months. Amzat and Allegra liked to sit on a bench beneath their grape arbor, in front of their small, cozy house. In the warm sunlight, beneath a peerless blue sky, they would count their blessings and share a peach.

But despite their felicity, they were so poor they had to take turns wearing the one pair of shoes they possessed. And to vary the sameness of their meals, Amzat had once traded five figs for a bit of sausage with a passing farmer. He hung the sausage by a string over the table. From time to time, while they ate their supper,

they would sniff the sausage, which allowed them to imagine that the pasta they always had was rich and savory.

It may seem unfair, but the custom in that part of the world was that the youngest brother never inherited gold. All Amzat had been left by his father was the top of the hill. But Ingrato and Bramoso had gotten their farm and the sheep as well as linen and furniture and gold pieces.

Alas, the two elder brothers were not content with their inheritance. They had steamed and boiled with rage for years, especially after they heard about Amzat and Allegra's fruit trees, the grape arbor, and the five olive trees, all of which flourished in the sunshine.

One morning, Furiosa and Tètra, who often spoke the same words at the same time, said, "We must get the hill away from Amzat and Allegra!"

"How can we do such a thing?" shouted Ingrato. "What an idiotic idea! I suppose you think we can put the hill in a wheelbarrow and trundle it down here to our valley!"

"Not at all," said Tètra. "Furiosa and I devised a plan some time ago. We will take the hill from them according to the law." She held up a document so soiled and creased it might have been lying at the bottom of some chest for years. "I have written this deed, and Furiosa had the wit to bury it in our table scraps this last month. The deed says that we are to be given the hill after five years from a certain date. Tomorrow is the end of the fifth year. You must show it to Amzat and Allegra and give them their walking papers."

"They won't believe it," protested Bramoso.

"Of course they'll believe it!" cried Tètra. "It is entirely legal since I have written your father's signature on it!"

The two brothers were not quite convinced the plan would work, but they summoned the old man who did odd jobs about the farm. They ordered him to deliver a message to Amzat — that they had discovered a deed that entitled them to the hill and that within two hours they were coming to take possession of it. The old man scrabbled up the hill, furious that he had been sent on such an errand. As he clutched at rocks and the roots of stunted trees, he brooded on the haughty way the two brothers and their wives always spoke to him. He thought of the knobby, angry little sheep that were always wandering off in search of food because the two brothers were too lazy to build fences to keep them in. He recalled how the brothers had not permitted him to wear his own father's fine cloak to the fair in the village miles away, lest he be taken for a landowner instead of the peasant he was.

But by the time he reached the summit of the hill and saw the small house, and Amzat and Allegra sitting on their bench eating figs, the sunlight had begun to warm him, first his thatch of white hair, then his neck, then his shoulders, then his entire self. A mysterious feeling of joy rose in him, so that he was actually smiling as he delivered the message from the two brothers and their wives.

After the old man had gone down the hill, Amzat and Allegra finished their figs and gazed wordlessly at each other for a long time.

In the sunny stillness, they heard the low mumble from a terra-cotta pot of beans that cooked all day long on the back of their stove.

These beans were as hard as pebbles, but the happy couple could afford little else besides the daily pasta.

The only variety in their daily fare was provided by the fruit. But of course, fruit did not grow in every season of the year.

At last, Amzat spoke. "I have a plan," he said.

As he explained to Allegra what was in his mind, she began to smile. Then they arose from their wooden bench and went inside their house to make preparations for the arrival of Ingrato and Bramoso.

Next to the kitchen was a small room with a floor made of bricks, where Allegra kept a broom, several bottles of olive oil pressed from their own olives, and a chest in which she stored their few worn but clean pieces of bed linen.

Amzat took four paces, which brought him to the center of the room. There, with the aid of an old chisel, he removed one brick from the floor. From the kitchen, Allegra carried in a copper bowl holding a few embers from the stove. She tipped them into the hole where the brick had been. Amzat then fetched the terra-cotta pot of beans and placed it so carefully over the hole filled with embers that they were perfectly hidden. Anyone would have thought the beans were cooking right there on the cold floor!

Amzat wrapped the brick in a rag and placed it in the chest on top of the linen. "We are ready," he said.

And only a little while later, the lighthearted couple heard Ingrato and Bramoso shouting threats as they clambered up the last few yards of the hill.

Amzat and Allegra waited in the small room where the bean pot steamed busily on the floor. The two elder brothers rushed into the room but halted when they caught sight of the pot.

"What is that?" cried Ingrato.

"Why, it is our magic pot," replied Amzat in an amiable voice. "It always cooks our beans to perfection."

"Imagine what a blessing that pot would be to our cranky wives," muttered Bramoso to Ingrato.

Allegra began to sing a pretty song about a dove, and Amzat capered around her as though neither of them had a care in the world.

The two brothers whispered together another moment. Then Ingrato spoke. "Stop that foolish singing and bobbing about, Amzat, and give us your pot. We'll forget about the deed for the time being," he said.

"Gladly," said Amzat. "But why don't you sit on our bench in the sunlight for a moment while I get everything ready."

The two brothers, pleased at the thought of a bit of warmth, even though it would remind them of how dank and dark their valley was, went outside. Amzat wrapped the terra-cotta pot in an old kerchief. Allegra quickly took the brick from the chest and put it back into the floor.

When Ingrato and Bramoso returned to their farmhouse, Furiosa and Tètra were reclining on their beds, sighing and complaining about all the work they had done while their husbands were away.

"Never mind all that!" shouted Ingrato. "Get up, you lazy creatures, and see what we've brought home for you!"

The wives joined their husbands in their storeroom, which had a brick floor like the one in Amzat's small room. There they kept sacks of feed, the sheep shears, farm tools, and odds and ends they had extorted, or stolen outright, from their few miserable tenants who lived in hovels at the furthest edges of the farm.

On top of a moldy, dusty pile of raggle-taggle clothing, a plump hen had made herself a deliciously comfortable nest. The two wives flew at the hen, screeching and

waving their arms, and she scurried in terror out of a window, vowing to herself never to lay a single egg for those devils, no matter what they gave her to eat.

"Did you show them the deed? When are they packing their rags and leaving? How soon can we move to the hill?" asked Tètra.

Ingrato said not a word, only unwrapped the still-warm terra-cotta pot of beans and placed it on the brick floor in the center of the storeroom.

Bramoso said, "Now you will see a thing you've never seen before."

"I see nothing but a disgusting old bean pot," screeched Furiosa. "I want my hill and my fruit trees and olive trees and grape arbor and sunshine!"

"Patience, my harridan of a sister-in-law," said Ingrato.

Bramoso turned fiery red. "How dare you speak to my wife in such an insulting way!" he cried. At once, the four of them began to quarrel and accuse one another of everything dreadful under the heavens.

But this sort of thing took place at least once every day, sometimes twice, and they were all quite accustomed to it. In less than two minutes, they had calmed down and were staring at the pot.

"What is it we are supposed to see?" asked Tètra in

what was for her a rather mild voice. "There's just an old pot sitting on the floor instead of in its proper place on the back of the stove."

"It's a magic pot," said Ingrato, "and it will cook the beans right there on the brick floor without anyone lifting a finger."

The four of them stared and stared at the pot. It did nothing, of course. Finally, Bramoso knelt and placed his hands against its sides, which were, by then, quite cold.

He looked at Ingrato. "Amzat and Allegra have made fools of us," he said, and began to grind his teeth so loudly in rage that one of the angry, knobby little sheep who had been searching near the farmhouse for something to eat, heard him through the window and trotted away as fast as she could for fear that the shearing was about to begin.

Bramoso clenched his huge fists and waved them in the air. "We've been duped!" he howled.

How the two wives laughed and laughed until their faces turned the color of tomato sauce.

"Idiots! Nincompoops! Noodleheads! Dunces!" they bawled. Ingrato gave a great kick and smashed the terra-cotta pot, and the hard beans flew up and then rained down like hailstones on the brick floor.

IN THE FARMHOUSE on the top of the very steep hill, Amzat and Allegra were preparing for the return of the two brothers. They knew that Ingrato and Bramoso would come back to claim the hill, waving the deed that the happy pair suspected was a sham, and that they would be twice as angry as before.

Now, Amzat and Allegra had two identical hares, which they kept as pets. One of the hares was called Luce, and the other Ombra. Allegra and Amzat could not tell them apart, but they had named the dear creatures out of love for them.

Very soon they heard Ingrato and Bramoso uttering terrible threats against them as they struggled up the hill.

"I will take Ombra to the meadow," said Amzat quickly. "When my brothers appear, do as I tell you."

A few minutes later, Ingrato and Bramoso came over the brow of the hill like two dark clouds rising from the valley below. Allegra stood before them in the sunlight, holding a glossy hare in her arms.

"Where is that scoundrel Amzat?" roared Ingrato.

"Where is that rascal?" thundered Bramoso.

"If only we had known you so longed to see him," Allegra said in her sweetest voice. "But wait a few short

moments, and I will send my hare, Luce, to fetch him
from the meadow where he is gathering herbs."

"No more fooling!" commanded Ingrato.

Allegra laughed her best cascading, silvery laugh.

Then she said, as she let the hare jump from her arms
to the ground, "Not at all! No fooling! You will see!"

The hare was disappearing into the tall grass as she
called to it, "Go, my Luce. Bring back Amzat!"

"What nonsense is this?" asked Bramoso. "Next, you

will be telling us you have a pet wolf that you send to the mill to buy flour."

"Only have patience," said Allegra. "Meanwhile, I have made a pot of the strong coffee we know you love." Allegra knew no such thing, but she hoped to flatter the brothers so they would calm down until Amzat's new plan was accomplished. She brought each of them a small cup of coffee that she had made from the very last beans she had.

Grumbling about having to wait and snorting about the very idea of a hare being able to carry a message to Amzat, the brothers each downed their coffee with a single swallow. By the time they had set down their empty cups on the bench, Amzat appeared before them, a hare in his arms.

"Luce came with a message that you wished to see me," he called out to his wife, who was standing in the doorway of the farmhouse. Then — as if just noticing the presence of his brothers — he added, "I am sure you understand that there is no point to my wife's coming to the meadow to get me when we have our Luce, our wonderful messenger."

"This is amazing," Bramoso whispered to Ingrato.

"Think of how happy our wives would be to have such a hare," whispered Ingrato to Bramoso.

Ingrato turned to the happy couple. "Give us that hare, and we will forget about the deed and the terra-cotta pot."

"Gladly," said Amzat, and handed over the hare, secretly wondering if it was Luce or Ombra.

As the two brothers vanished down the hill, Allegra and Amzat clasped hands and danced around their bench beneath the grape arbor.

THAT AFTERNOON, Ingrato and Bramoso, after giving their wives instructions, left the hare with them and went off to their field to work.

As the sky turned rose and violet, the brothers began to cast eager glances toward the farmhouse. "Soon the little hare will come to tell us it is time to go home," Ingrato said with satisfaction.

The sky darkened until it held one last streak of light like a golden spear. Then the heavens grew black and slowly filled with the glimmer of the distant stars.

At the farmhouse, an hour earlier, Furiosa had dropped the hare to the ground. "It will soon be dark," she said. "Go and fetch your masters."

Luce, of course, made for the top of the very steep hill; her twin, Ombra; and their gentle owners.

"I'm so cold!" Bramoso bellowed into the night silence.

A faint bleating seemed to mock him.

"I'm so hungry!" howled Ingrato. A loud *hee-haw* seemed to jeer at him.

When the pale light of morning began to steal across the valley, leaving it almost at once because of the shadow of the very steep hill, the earliest birds observed the two brothers stumbling, and cursing like madmen, as they neared the farmhouse.

Inside, they found their wives asleep at the kitchen table, their heads resting on their arms in the flickering light of a stub of candle.

"Wake up!" cried Ingrato. "What have you done with that hare?"

It took them only a second to realize that once again they had been tricked by Amzat and Allegra.

"AND NOW," Amzat said to his wife, "we must come up with the greatest plan of all."

It happened that on that very morning, Amzat had killed the pig they had been fattening up all year for their New Year's feast. After certain preparations, Amzat came to Allegra, who was brushing the glossy coats of Luce and Ombra, and said, "Do you see what I am holding? It is the pig's intestine, which I have filled with blood. You must wear it beneath the waistband of your darkest skirt. When we hear my brothers approaching, do as I tell you."

They went to wait on their bench beneath the grape arbor. All too soon, they heard Ingrato and Bramoso fuming and growling as they hastened up the hill.

At once, Amzat and Allegra began to shout insults at each other. As soon as the two brothers appeared over the brow of the hill, Amzat seized a huge kitchen knife that was lying on the bench and stabbed Allegra. The earth turned red with the pig's blood as Allegra sank to the ground with a mournful cry.

Ingrato and Bramoso, who had observed the terrible scene with mouths agape, cried, "You are crack-brained! You are moonstruck!"

Amzat laughed aloud. "Oh, we often amuse ourselves in this fashion," he said, flourishing the knife. "This is not an ordinary knife. Listen and watch!" And at once, he began to intone these words:

"White knife, quick knife,
Glittering, cursed,
The life you have taken,
Give back to us."

As Amzat pronounced the word *life*, Allegra rose from the ground, and husband and wife embraced each other.

"We must have that knife," Ingrato whispered to Bramoso. "Think how we can scare our bad-tempered wives!"

"Give us the knife," Bramoso commanded the joyful couple, "and we will forget the deed to the hill — for the time being — and the outrageous tricks you've played upon us."

"Gladly," replied Amzat. "But be sure you remember the magic verse!"

Ingrato and Bramoso went off down the hill, hardly able to wait until they could pick a quarrel with their wives.

In that household, of course, it was an easy matter.

In no time at all, the four of them were stamping their feet on the floor and exchanging the rudest remarks anyone could imagine.

Suddenly, with a quick wink at Bramoso, Ingrato took the knife from his belt and stabbed Furiosa and Tètra.

Bramoso chanted the magic verse.

The wives did not come back to life.

When Ingrato and Bramoso realized what had happened, they didn't waste a second. Ingrato grabbed up a great sack in their storeroom, emptied it of grain, and the two of them set off for the very steep hill, running faster than the wind.

When they reached the summit, they found Amzat picking figs from his tree. They threw him into the sack while Allegra wept in the doorway and wrung her hands.

AMZAT WAS a heavy burden, but rage had given the brothers great strength. They carried him down the hill, past their farmhouse, and to a stone bridge that spanned a boisterous torrent that flowed through the valley.

Their exertions had exhausted them. They were obliged to descend to the banks of the stream and douse their heads in water.

Meanwhile, Amzat, his arms and legs all tumbled together in the grain sack, heard the baaing of a flock of sheep, which was, at that very moment, crossing the bridge.

He began to howl at the top of his lungs, "They want me to marry the King's daughter, with all her gold and jewels, and live in the great castle. But, oh! Oh! I don't want to marry her at all."

The shepherd of the flock, who was just then walking past the sack, leaned on his tall shepherd's crook and began to smile broadly.

"I would love to marry the King's daughter, with all her gold and jewels, and live with her in the great castle," he said.

In a second, Amzat and the shepherd exchanged places.

The two brothers, refreshed and burning to take their

revenge on Amzat, returned to the bridge, snatched up the sack, and hurled the unsuspecting shepherd into the torrent.

"Justice has been done," said Ingrato.

No sooner had the words left his mouth than the brothers heard a familiar voice singing a song about a nightingale.

Not far ahead of them, on the other side of the bridge, on the road that led to the distant village, they saw a large flock of sheep. In the midst of the flock, carrying the shepherd's crook, stood their brother, Amzat.

"This cannot be!" exclaimed Bramoso.

"He belongs to the devil's party," muttered Ingrato as the two of them hastened to catch up with Amzat.

"Ah . . . here you are," Amzat said, smiling at them genially. "Just the two people I most wanted to see! This torrent we have crossed is a wonder. As soon as I floated down to the bottom, a great flock of sheep surrounded me. I would have been here sooner, but I wanted to select the fattest sheep, and that took several seconds. Just look at the torrent! Look at the white foam! It shows that there are even more sheep trotting downstream, stirring up the waters on the streambed."

"Is this really the truth?" asked Bramoso in a voice full of suspicion.

"But you can see with your own eyes!" cried Amzat, waving his crook over the flock around him. "Where else could I have found these beauties?"

Ingrato looked greedily at the flock. "What must we do to get such fine sheep?" he asked.

"It's the easiest thing in the world," replied Amzat, who by then had seen a discarded wine cask by the side of the road. "If you merely jump into the torrent, the sheep will run away from you. But if you get into that cask, they will not see you, and you will be able to herd them out of the water."

The three brothers returned to the bridge. Ingrato and Bramoso, grumbling a little at the sour smell that rose from the bottom of the cask, climbed into it. With a great heave, Amzat lifted up the cask and dropped it into the bubbling water below.

All the rest of that day, on the top of the very steep hill, Amzat and Allegra sat beneath their grape arbor, the bright blue sky above them, bathed in the warm, sweet sunlight, and ate figs from their tree, which seemed to have increased its fruit one hundredfold.

Mezgalten

ONCE UPON A TIME, there lived a rooster who was so very tiny he was called Mezgalten, which means "half a rooster."

One fine morning, Mezgalten decided to take a walk to an acorn tree that stood on a small knoll at the edge of the farm where he lived.

As he was standing there in the shade beneath the tree, one leg curled up, a position he much enjoyed, and gazing out over the countryside, an acorn fell directly on his head.

He realized at once that he must see the world before it was too late. So he set off, leaving behind him the familiar land where he had been hatched from a tiny egg no larger than a grape.

He passed herds of grazing cattle and great stone

barns. He passed tall stooks of hay. He passed an ancient temple whose roofless columns stood like sentries in a field of stones. He passed through a stone village where all the shutters were locked and not a single voice could be heard.

Just beyond the village, he came across the first living thing he had met, a large white ewe sitting by the side of the road, weeping tears as big as pearls.

"Whatever makes you cry so hard?" asked Mezgalten.

"The wolf! The wolf!" sobbed the ewe. "Oh, the wolf has taken my two little kids, and I know he has eaten them all up!"

"But how did such a dreadful thing happen?" Mezgalten asked, for ever since the acorn had hit him on the head, he had felt an immense curiosity about everything under the sun.

"It was this way," answered the ewe, wiping her eyes and gasping as she spoke. "I had left them at home to go to a neighboring farm where I give my milk to be made into cheese. I told my little ones that if they heard a knock on the door, they were to look through a crack at the bottom to make sure they saw my white feet."

And here she broke into pitiful sobs once again.

"Go on, go on," urged Mezgalten, for his newly awakened curiosity had made him somewhat impatient.

The ewe gulped twice and continued.

"But the wolf is so clever! He wrapped his front paws in white laundry cord, and so when my poor little innocent kids looked through the crack, they thought it was me, their dear mother!"

"What a heartrending story," Mezgalten said. "I think you should join me to see the world before it is too late. Perhaps there will be a surprise or two."

So Mezgalten and the ewe walked together along the road. They passed a vineyard where vines, strung between small fruit trees, held clusters of grapes. They passed through a vast field of drooping sunflowers. They passed through a grove of olive trees whose trunks seemed to twist and turn like dancers. They passed a dark castle whose great iron gates were locked. They passed three horses as pale as wheat who galloped together in a narrow pasture.

Just beyond the pasture, they saw a donkey stamping his feet in a ditch and shouting up at the sky.

When they reached the donkey, Mezgalten asked, "Whatever makes you shout up at the sky and stamp the ground?"

"I would also like to know," remarked the ewe, who was feeling slightly more cheerful because of the company of the tiny rooster.

"I've been sacked, let go, left without a means of earning my living. That's what's happened!" cried the donkey.

The ewe observed to herself that the donkey's trouble wasn't worth a bean compared to her own. Still, she found she couldn't help but be interested in his story.

"How did such a thing come about?" she asked shyly.

"It happened in this way," began the donkey. "I was carrying two sacks of chestnuts to the village for my master when a four-footed monster, wrapped in horrible, filthy rags that blew in the wind and frightened me, jumped out from behind a tree and made off with the

sacks. When I arrived in the village without them, my master kicked me and beat me and told me to take myself off. Now you see the miserable fix I am in."

"Well, then, you'd better come along with us to see the world before it is too late," said Mezgalten. "Who knows?" he added. "There might be a surprise or two along the way."

The tiny rooster, the ewe, and the donkey continued along the road. They passed four brick towers the color of orange marmalade. On the tallest of the towers stood an old man who stared up at the sun, his arms held out like wings. They passed a field of tall grass where three old women, bent like pins, seemed to search the ground for something lost. They passed a steep hill on the very top of which sat a gray monastery that was like a ship of stone about to sail off into the air. On a distant hillside, they saw a flock of grazing sheep that looked like separate grains of rice.

"What is that in the road ahead?" asked the donkey.

"It's lying flat in the dust," remarked the ewe.

"It's a one-eyed cat," said Mezgalten.

The cat's head was resting on its front paws. It stared at them out of its one unblinking eye.

"Why are you lying in the road like an old shoe?" asked Mezgalten.

"Why do you have only one good eye?" asked the donkey, who was frequently rude, though he never intended to be.

"And why are you so dusty?" asked the ewe, who prided herself on being tidy and clean.

The cat rose to her full height and arched her back.

"This is my story," she began. "I was passing the time of day with a wolf — speaking of the weather and other such matters — when the wicked creature had a fit of some kind and threw himself at me. I fought with all my strength, but I lost my eye."

"I think you had better come along with us and see the world before it is too late," said Mezgalten. "Perhaps there will be surprises awaiting all of us," he added.

So Mezgalten, the ewe, the donkey, and the cat with one eye continued along the road.

They passed a large cistern full of water in which shone a reflection of the purpling sky. They passed three cooing doves, who paced across the roof of a collapsed shed on their ruby feet. They passed a sloping meadow in which red flowers swayed in a slight breeze. They crossed a small stone bridge over a lively stream that mumbled and whispered as it flowed over stones that looked like pale, round loaves of bread.

"There is something limping and swaying ahead of us down the road," said the ewe.

"I believe it is a dog," said the donkey.

"Let sleeping dogs lie," said the cat.

"It isn't asleep," said the donkey.

"I hope it won't bark at us," said Mezgalten. "Barking makes my tail feathers quiver."

But the dog, who had turned to stare at the four animals as they approached him, uttered not a sound.

"How bedraggled you are," said the donkey.

"You do look a bit worse for wear," said the ewe.

The cat said nothing.

"I hope you were not caught in an olive press," said Mezgalten.

The dog shook his head. When he spoke, his voice was like gravel flowing over nails.

"I have been in the most dreadful fight," he uttered hoarsely. "A wolf, dressed in disgusting rags and tatters, came hurtling down a hill and flung himself at me. I barked so much I have used up my barking. I am, in fact, a wreck."

The donkey said, "But it must be the same wolf that stole my chestnuts!"

"And ate my kids!" said the ewe.

"And blinded me in one eye!" cried the cat.

"I think you had better join us," Mezgalten advised the dog, "and see the world before it is too late. Who can tell what great surprises await us all?"

So Mezgalten, the ewe, the donkey, the cat, and the dog went on down the road.

By then, night had begun to fall. The cat, squinting its one eye, paused by the side of the road to look at a small sign shaped like an arrow. " '*A forest,*' " she read aloud to her companions.

"And there it is just ahead," said the donkey. "What a thick, black forest! Surely we'll get lost!"

"Perhaps we'll be able to find some shelter among the trees," said Mezgalten.

"And perhaps we won't," rasped the dog.

"Could you make your way up a tree and see what you can see?" the ewe asked the tiny rooster.

"I'll do my best," promised Mezgalten.

"Be sure to look right, look left, look behind you and in front of you," advised the donkey.

"Naturally," said Mezgalten, and flapping his wings rapidly, he flew to the top of a small pine tree.

"Do you see anything?" called up the cat.

"Yes, I see nothing," answered Mezgalten.

"How can you see *nothing*?" asked the ewe.

"By concentrating," said Mezgalten.

"And now?" asked the dog. "Do you see something?"

"Now I see a faint glimmer in the middle of the forest. I do believe it is a burning candle. If it is a candle, there will be a window. If there is a window, there must be a house," said the tiny rooster.

Mezgalten flew down to join the ewe, the donkey, the cat, and the dog. "Let us set off to find the house before we are found by the creatures that hunt for their dinners in the pit of the night," he said.

So the little group made their way among the trees until they came to a clearing in which stood a most curious small house. It was made of stones and roots and the branches of trees, all piled up, all jumbled together, and tied here and there with a thick white rope. In the window, a candle flame flickered like a yellow moth.

"The door is open," whispered the cat.

"Whoever built this house has an untidy mind," commented the ewe.

"Perhaps it is inhabited," said the donkey.

"Perhaps we are being watched," growled the dog.

"It is too late to go back," said Mezgalten. "We must be brave and go forward."

No sooner had the tiny rooster led his friends into the house than he felt chicken feathers around his feet. "I don't care for these feathers," he said. "They make me wonder where the chickens have gone."

"Never mind," said the donkey. "At least we have a roof over our heads. But this is only the room where the livestock is kept. We must climb those stairs in the corner."

On hoof and paw and toe, the five comrades ascended the flight of narrow stone steps to a closed door. The donkey butted it with his long head until it opened into a room lit with the golden light of a candle that stood in a window.

A clock ticked on a mantel over a hearth. A chest stood near the window. On the floor lay a straw pallet covered with grimy, dusty, nasty rags. On the wall above the pallet hung a portrait. The animals gathered to stare up at it.

Across the bottom, in letters written with many flourishes and curlicues, was the word *Grandmother*. And staring down at them, wearing a bright red gypsy scarf, was a very old wolf, her long fangs gleaming like icicles.

"But this must be the house of the wolf!" cried Mezgalten in alarm.

"Lock the doors! Lock the window! Stuff stones up the chimney!" shouted the donkey.

"It is a good thing we have seen some of the world," said the cat, "because now it is surely too late!"

Grandmother

"Let us flee," grated the dog.

But the ewe said, "We have no time to flee. I sense danger nearby, all the way to my little white bones."

At her words, which all the animals believed at once, Mezgalten flew to the top of the clock. The cat ran to the hearth and crouched among the ashes, her good eye opened wide. The dog blew out the candle and jumped on the chest. The ewe stood at the top of the stairs. And the donkey, after banging shut the door with his rear hooves, clattered down to the room below, where he stood among the drifting heaps of chicken feathers.

As soon as they had all taken their places, they heard the wolf at the door, snarling and gnashing his great teeth. He tore up the stairs, and when he found the door closed, he let out the most tremendous roar and threw himself against it, bursting into the room, which was now as dark as the night outside.

"Where is my candle?" he shouted. "How dare it go out?" Then, catching sight of the cat's eye in the hearth and mistaking it for an ember, he grumbled, "At least, I can warm myself."

No sooner had he reached the hearth than the cat leaped on his muzzle and hung on with all her sharp claws. In terror, the wolf backed toward the stairs, trying to open his mouth to howl. Then Mezgalten flew to his head, digging his taloned toes into the thick pelt. The wretched wolf fell to the floor, whereupon the ewe jumped on him and raked him with her cloven hooves.

With Mezgalten like two hundred thorns on his head, with the cat still hanging on to his muzzle with all four of her paws, the wolf tumbled down the stairs. The donkey, waiting below, leaped upon him with all his weight. Meanwhile, the dog, his voice fully restored, ran this way and that, barking at his loudest.

"The wolf is dead," announced the donkey. The dog raced down the flight of stairs to join the ewe, the cat,

Mezgalten, and the triumphant donkey. In the pale light of the newly risen moon that shone on the curious small house in the clearing in the forest, the animals gazed down at what resembled an old gray carpet — except for the white fangs.

"Listen!" cried the ewe suddenly.

As though it came from a great distance, everyone heard a very faint bleating.

With her hoof, the ewe cut the wolf open. Out tumbled her two little kids.

"Mama!" they both cried joyfully.

There was great rejoicing and much crowing, meowing, bleating, barking, and hee-hawing. The candle was lit again. The dog, investigating the chest, found the donkey's two sacks of chestnuts.

"If someone would only find my eye," said the cat somewhat mournfully.

"I will be your eye," said Mezgalten.

"We will all be your eye," joined in the donkey, the ewe, and even the dog.

"Perhaps we have seen enough of the world," suggested the ewe.

"Perhaps it will never be too late to see more of it," said Mezgalten thoughtfully, adding, "or possibly it will be. In any event, I think this is as good a place as any to settle down and see what happens. But we must do several things first."

The donkey and the dog dragged the wolf, and the portrait of Grandmother Wolf in her red kerchief, off to a deeper part of the forest and buried both beneath the pine needles. The ewe and her little kids blew the chicken feathers out of the house and into the clearing, where they slowly floated to the ground. The cat cleaned out the ashes from the hearth. And Mezgalten, of course, made sure that all the animals' tasks were properly done.

Afterward, they had a fine feast of chestnuts and then they settled down to rest after their long day of seeing the world.

Olimpia, Cucol, and the Door

ON EVERY DAY of the year except New Year's, the villagers of Beffardo gathered at the village fountain to gossip and trade stories about Olimpia and her son, Cucol. These two lived in a hovel on the outskirts of Beffardo in a field where nothing grew except useless weeds, poppies, and vipers.

Most of the stories had been told so often they were as threadbare as cloth dipped a thousand times in the water of the stream that meandered through Beffardo and slapped a thousand times on the great flat rock where the women of the village knelt to wash and scrub their linen.

But where there is spite, new details can always be invented.

Only yesterday, the old man who made his own fiery

grappa and gave away not one drop of the brandy, even to his kin, reported that Olimpia had invited her pig, Tommaso, to sit at the table for the daily meal.

"What! They've given my brother's name to a pig?" cried the village miser.

"They are too ignorant to eat at a proper table," shrieked a crone who had put a curse on her neighbor's

goats to make them barren. "Cucol is so backward he is unable to imagine how to sit on a chair and, instead, squats on the ground like a dog!"

The Podestà, the headman of Beffardo, cleared his throat loudly. Everyone grew quiet, for he was the most cunning teller of tales about Olimpia and Cucol in the whole village.

"Cucol does not know who his own father is," he began. "I had heard recently that he rushes out to the road whenever a man passes by, calling him *Papa* and embracing him. How could I believe such an outrageous thing! Then, my little son, Ciacco, who is, as you all know, only nine years old, was on his way to the flour mill this week when, as he was passing by the field, Cucol hastened toward him, his arms held out, crying, '*Papa!* It is you!' "

The villagers were silent with shock at Cucol's foolishness, and also with the secret joy each felt at this new tattle they could chew over for at least a week.

The oldest story — which the villagers never tired of embroidering — concerned the rumor that Olimpia and Cucol had never taken a bath in their entire lives.

"Is it decent when you can recognize people before you can see them?" asked the miser, who had never done a decent thing in his life.

"Hee, hee," screeched the crone. "Even my dear little goats rush into the barn when Olimpia and Cucol are as far as a whole kilometer away!"

Poor Cucol! Poor Olimpia! Of course there was a little bit of truth in the stories that were told about them.

Out of affection for their old pig, whom they could never bring themselves to kill though they were often hungry, they had given him a name. It was not Tommaso but Paffuto.

They did have a table of sorts. It had only three legs, so they had to prop it up with stones.

Cucol was not backward, only very slow in reaching a conclusion, and as is true for most people, it was often the wrong one. But to Cucol a thought was an amazing thing, a beautiful cloud of meaning that he liked to study for a long time before he tried to make sense of it.

On rainy days, he did muse about who his father had been. Since he could not recall ever seeing him, his musing would cease when the rain did. But he would never have thrown his arms around strangers, for fear of embarrassing them. As for the Podestà's son, Cucol, seeing the little boy trudging wearily along the road under the hot midday sun, had merely gone to ask him if he would like a cooling drink.

The rumor in Beffardo that came closest to the truth

was that Olimpia and Cucol had never bathed in their lives. Olimpia believed that water, except when used in cooking or sipped for refreshment, could drown a person even if only applied to the face with a damp rag. When on some errand Olimpia was obliged to cross the stone bridge that spanned the village stream, she always made a magical sign with two fingers of her right hand to prevent the babbling water from leaping out of its bed and pouring down on her. But one day, she did venture near it.

The evening before, she had observed that Cucol's trousers were so encrusted with dirt, they stood up on the floor by themselves when he stepped out of them before pulling on his nightshirt. The next morning, she

carried them to the stream — they were as heavy as lead — and flung them in. As they sank into the clear water, dozens of little fish, accustomed to dine on the soap bubbles that usually rose when the village women rinsed their linen, swam eagerly to the surface. No sooner were they in the vicinity of Cucol's trousers than their bellies turned up. They were as dead as stones.

Olimpia and Cucol were unaware of the terrifying smell that accompanied them everywhere they went. As for the haste with which the villagers of Beffardo grabbed and pinched their own noses when Olimpia spoke to them, she knew they were peculiar folk and gave it not another thought.

But even she was bewildered when, during a sweltering August day, as she kneaded flour and salt and water for pasta and the sweat from her efforts fell in streams, the dough suddenly changed into marble.

"Amazing!" she murmured as she looked down at the golden stony mass. Twice more she began to knead the dough. Each time it turned into marble.

"It is some miraculous property that comes from the water in my body," she told herself. "What a puzzle! Water either drowns you or makes marble pasta!"

So she rose in the middle of the night, when the sun was on the other side of the world and the air was cool, and kneaded the dough very slowly. This time, the pasta formed properly. She cut the dough into strips and hung these over a string to dry. Just as she finished her labor and was yearning for her bed and sleep, she heard a roar of voices like a sudden rise of wind.

She ran to the door and peeked through a crack. By the light of the moon, she saw the villagers of Beffardo gathered on the road below the field.

Such shouting and chanting! Such stamping of feet! Were they bewitched? Olimpia wondered.

The villagers had convinced themselves that Cucol had tried to throttle the Podestà's son, Ciacco. The Podestà had declared that Olimpia and Cucol were a menace and had to be sent packing. You might say that the villagers had bewitched themselves.

Ciacco was, naturally, delighted with the attention and didn't mention that Cucol had only offered him a cooling drink of lemon and water.

The miser and the crone began to heave stones at the hovel. The rest of the villagers shouted hideous threats: they would hang Cucol; they would hurl Olimpia into the stream; they would burn down the hovel and roast the poor old pig.

Ciacco, giddy with his new importance, began to invent new details, crying out in his shrill little voice,

"Cucol has a pet wolf he commanded to eat me up! He tied a rope around my ankle and dangled me over a cliff!" But even these villagers could not believe everything. No one, they knew, had ever made a pet out of a wolf. And there wasn't a cliff within a hundred kilometers of Beffardo.

"Close your mouth, you wretch!" the Podestà whispered angrily to his son. By then, the quickly bored people were dropping their stones and had begun to make their way back to the village.

Olimpia, crouching behind the door, her heart beating as rapidly as the heart of a small beast in the forest pursued by an owl, knew she had had enough of Beffardo and its hateful inhabitants.

She woke up Cucol. "Let the pig loose," she said. "He can forage for himself, poor old fellow, and may be glad for his freedom. You and I are leaving this very night. Where we will end up, I can't say. But it cannot help but be better than this place."

She gathered their few possessions into an old kerchief and tied the corners into a knot. She closed the shutters of the window. She snuffed the candle. As she went out into the night, she called back over her shoulder, "Cucol, take care of the door."

Though she was neither glad nor sad to abandon the place where she had lived with her son for so many years, she meant to leave it in order.

She set off through the field without fear of the vipers that lived among the poppies and useless weeds. Why should she fear them? She had never stamped her foot at one or chased it with a stick or called it a vile name. Live and let live was her motto.

Because she was so accustomed to Cucol following her, she did not trouble to look behind herself.

Cucol was not following her. He was thinking about the old wooden door. Having considered Olimpia's words, "Take care of the door," he had decided she meant to take it with them.

And it was a good idea, wasn't it? If there was a storm, they could shelter beneath it. If there was a river to ford, they could use it as a raft. Having convinced himself of what he must do, Cucol gripped the door with his two huge hands and pulled and pushed and heaved until it came loose from its rusty old hinges.

Slinging it on his back, Cucol now hurried after his mother, who was already walking quickly down the road.

Olimpia was certain the villagers would return to abuse them, if not tomorrow, then the next day. She resolved that she and Cucol would take shelter in the great forest, the tops of whose oak and pine trees she had often glimpsed from the hovel on clear days. When she turned back to tell Cucol her plan, she saw her son bent under the weight of the door, puffing as he tried to keep up with her.

"You great silly! Why are you carrying the door?" she asked. But she didn't wait for an answer. She knew all too well the winding paths along which her son's

thoughts could meander. And there was no time to waste.

"Never mind! Over this wall! We'll hide in the forest. By next week, those Beffardo geese may have forgotten us."

They clambered over the stone wall — a struggle for Cucol bent double under the weight of the door — then skirted a field of ripe corn and, in another two minutes, entered the dark forest.

How cold and still it was! "We must be in a space between two stars," muttered Cucol. Then there was a rustle of leaves, a loud squeak, a scrabble of claws on bark, and the beating of wings.

Olimpia's heart thumped with dread. How she longed for the hovel, for shutters she could close against the night, for a door she could bolt. And now all she had was a door!

"Stop panting," she implored Cucol. "I hear something!"

Underbrush whispered. Twigs crackled. Feet pounded on the forest floor. Worst of all was the rise and fall of voices.

"The villagers have come after us. There is nothing to do but climb!" Olimpia whispered, and seizing the lower branches of the nearest tree, she began to ascend it rapidly, limb by limb. Cucol followed her up as best as he could, the door banging against the trunk of the tree and twisting and dipping and rising like a wild horse. But Cucol's grip did not weaken for one instant.

Where the thick trunk divided into two forks, Olimpia's hands touched a large, smooth hollow. She reached back, under the door, and grabbed a handful of Cucol's hair. "Settle in here as quietly as you can," she ordered him.

"Is this our new home?" wondered Cucol aloud as he held the door over their heads like a roof.

"It may well be our new home if we don't survive this new trial the devil has sent," muttered Olimpia.

The voices she had heard now turned into thunderous shouts as three thieves gathered at the base of the tree to divide an enormous sack of gold they had stolen only a few hours earlier. And no sooner had one of them loosened the cord that bound the sack than they fell into a violent quarrel. Almost at once, harsh words turned into furious blows.

Such caterwauling, such threats and curses rose from the base of the tree like the flames of a fierce fire reaching ever higher, that Cucol began to tremble, and all around, the branches and the smallest twigs began to quiver. Olimpia patted his brow. She pinched his arms. She pulled his ears. But his shaking grew greater, and as was bound to happen, his grip on the door loosened at last.

With a terrible *whoosh!* — a sound like the wings of the angel of strife and death — the door crashed through the branches of the tree and smashed to earth.

The three thieves howled in terror and, without a second's thought for their stolen treasure, fled in three different directions.

Silence returned to the forest as Olimpia and Cucol

descended the tree to the ground, a far easier journey than their ascent had been.

Olimpia dipped her hands into the sack and brought up masses of gold pieces.

"Our fate has taken a turn," she said to Cucol.

Cucol nodded as he usually did when his mother spoke, whether he had listened closely to her or not.

"A door has surprising uses," he said slowly. "But I am thinking of how cold and hungry I am."

"Soon you won't be," Olimpia said. Lifting the sack to her back, she set off out of the forest to the road. This time, she glanced behind her. Cucol was bending to lift the door.

"Leave it there in the forest where it began its life as a tiny acorn," she said. "It has served us well."

SOME TIME LATER, in a shining city filled with extensive gardens, grand piazzas, and statues that looked alive, Olimpia and Cucol lived in a palace. The walls of their great salon were covered with wine red silk. The candles in glittering chandeliers were kept lighted day and night. Mother and son dined whenever they felt hungry. A large staff of servants carried out their smallest whim.

The most important people of the city came to visit and to stuff themselves from the vast variety of glorious dishes that were always spread out upon long tables. A few of them, when they were short of money, helped themselves to one or two of the many precious objects that lay about on tables. Still, no matter how often they called upon Olimpia and Cucol, they kept at a distance from them, speaking, when their mouths weren't crammed with food, from a doorway or next to an open window.

Olimpia and Cucol had not, as yet, learned the delights of bathing.

One late afternoon, a learned philosopher from the city's ancient university came to visit. He pointed to an immense golden tub in one of the smaller reception rooms.

"Why have you filled that tub with polenta?" he asked.

"Because my son, Cucol, loves polenta above all things and cannot get enough of it," replied Olimpia. "The poor boy went without it for so many years. Now he has it whenever he wishes."

"There are different ways of looking at a thing," the philosopher said. "For example, this tub you have filled with polenta can also be used for bathing."

"Bathing!" cried Olimpia, shuddering. "You must mean *drowning*."

"Not at all," said the philosopher. "Do the fish in the sea drown? Have you not observed the city boys jumping from the bridge to bathe in the river? I myself bathe weekly and find it a delicious experience."

After further gentle arguments, Olimpia, who held the professor in the greatest esteem, was persuaded to venture into the tub after it was emptied of polenta and filled with perfumed water.

In no time at all, she was cavorting in the tub like a

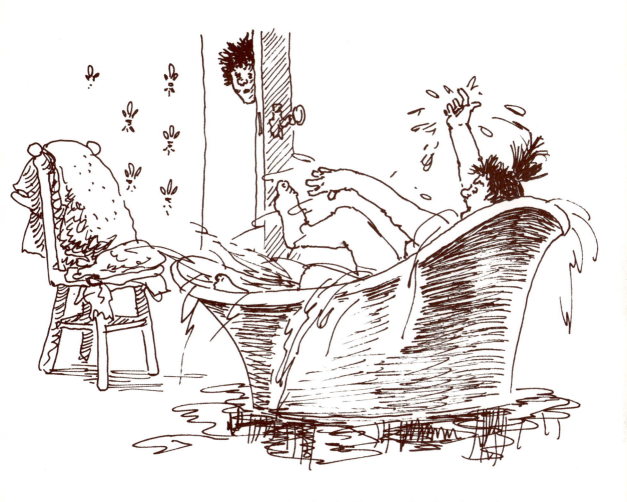

city boy in the river. Cucol, who had never had a thought about the subject, also took a bath.

Very soon, the important people who thronged the palace day and night grew much friendlier. Olimpia felt that if attaining the gold had done nothing else but lead her into water, it had been a great stroke of fortune.

Back in Beffardo, life had also changed. Most of the villagers missed Olimpia and Cucol. Who were they to gossip about? Who could they jeer at to cheer themselves up?

After some speculation, it was agreed by all that Olimpia and Cucol had been eaten by wolves, though no wolves had been seen in the area for a hundred years. But of course, people can believe whatever they want to believe.

In any event, it was not long before they found something new with which to occupy themselves.

A transformation had taken place in the characters of the Podestà, the crone who cast spells, the old man who made the fiery *grappa*, and the miser. They had never been agreeable, but of late they had become so bad tempered, so given to wild rages, that the villagers ran away from them, no matter how much they might need the Podestà's advice, a spell from the crone, a sip of *grappa* from the old man, or a loan at high interest from the miser.

In fact, these leading citizens of Beffardo grew so hateful that one stormy night when the rain fell in torrents and the wind blew black clouds across the sky, the villagers drove them away, along with Ciacco, the Podestà's son.

The crone, the old man, the miser, the Podestà, and Ciacco, desperate for shelter in such a tempest, found one soon enough in the very hovel where Olimpia and Cucol had once lived.

But no sooner had they a roof over their heads and a dry earthen floor beneath their feet than they all burst into loud lamentation. As each confessed before that night was over, they had lost a fortune it had taken them years to amass, the old man and the crone from selling *grappa* and wicked spells all around the countryside, the miser from his money lending, and the Podestà from stealing everything he could lay his hands on from his miserable tenant farmers as well as from the village treasury.

No one in Beffardo had known of those hidden stores. And no one, of course, knew that the sack the three thieves had left at the base of the tree in which Olimpia and Cucol had concealed themselves, had held all the gold that had belonged to the four who had been exiled from the village.

They lived on together in the hovel for many years, each one claiming his loss was far greater than that of the other three.

In fact, their hours were so filled with complaint that not one of them would spare the time it would have taken to replace the door that Cucol had torn from its hinges on that night so long ago. Rain, snow, wind, and even clods of earth blew through the hole where the door had been, and soon enough there was hardly any difference between indoors and outdoors. Not that the Podestà, the old man, the crone, or the miser would have noticed.

In time, Ciacco grew weary of the ceaseless grumbling and ran away from the hovel to a distant kingdom where, eventually, he became the favorite storyteller of a bored and aged king. But that is another story.

It is likely that Cucol, if he had put his mind to it, could have figured out where the gold had come from that had changed his and Olimpia's life.

But it was not a subject that interested him. Anyhow, his mind was now completely taken up with a princess he was thinking of marrying.

Also by Paula Fox

MONKEY ISLAND

THE VILLAGE BY THE SEA

LILY AND THE LOST BOY

THE MOONLIGHT MAN

ONE-EYED CAT

A PLACE APART

THE SLAVE DANCER

BLOWFISH LIVE IN THE SEA

PORTRAIT OF IVAN

THE STONE-FACED BOY

HOW MANY MILES TO BABYLON?